The Destiny Ring

A Story of Pine Mountain

Chloe Sanguine

To the one who has made me believe there really is a heaven on earth, and it's Pine Mountain, Georgia. I will forever hold a special place in my heart for you! There is no goodbye, it's until we meet again.

To Pine Mountain, Georgia… and everyone who made this book possible…

Chapter One

"Where were you today, Geneva?" My friend Gladys reaches for the nearest coffee pot and pours herself a cup. The steam from her cup makes her cheeks flush as she takes a sip.

"I went to Pine Mountain!"

Shocked, her cup clicks against the table as she re positions herself in her chair!

"You haven't been there in years, my friend. You haven't even been outside this retirement home." She takes another sip from her cup and gently brushes the table with her hand where sugar granules had collected from the previous guest.

"Oh I was really there, Gladys. I mean, I was actually THERE and not in my dreams."

Gladys gave me a sad look and asks "What is so special about Pine Mountain? It's just a little town in Georgia I mean... come on, what happened to you there? Why do you keep GOING there?"

"Oh Gladys, I knew someone very special who lived there and I haven't seen him in well over 30 years now. I still think about him all the time, but I never thought about looking him up. I've just been too shy. The last time I saw him it didn't end well and I never spoke to him again after that and... There have been times when I've thought about looking him up... but I never did!"

"Geneva!" Gladys puts her cup down on the table and takes both of my hands. "Geneva, you have to forget about that memory. It seems like you loved that guy very much, but there are things you have to overcome... You have the life you wanted, what more could you ever ASK for? The past is just a MEMORY and you need to let that go."

Sadly, I looked downward "Have I ever told you the story of The Destiny Ring?" Gladys wrinkles her forehead "No, you haven't, what's it about?"

I get up out of my chair and walk over to the coffee station and pour me a cup. The steam drifted around me like a light mist as I quickly return to my table and sit down. I clear my throat and pull out my leather pouch. The eagle on it was missing its eye. I reach down into it and pull out a beautiful sparkling ring. A teardrop aquamarine jewel sparkles against mother of pearl with silver embedded accents.

"Wow" Gladys remarks, "What kind of ring is that?"

"It's The Destiny Ring." I say. "This ring has a story behind it and I've had it a very long time. I made a promise that I would treasure it all my life. Someone very special gave it to me and I keep it with me wherever I go."

Gladys gave me a hard look, "Again! You're dwelling again, Geneva!"

I sit back in my chair and say "Now I will tell you a beautiful story about this ring. It was the middle of June. Carson and I had been talking a lot. I traveled to Pine Mountain to see him. All the shops were open. We walk down a brick sidewalk."

"I'm playing at Gayla's Gift Shop on Friday and Saturday." he says.

"Is that a restaurant?" I ask.

Carson replies, "It's a country store. My friend Gayla runs it. I've known her all my life."

"Oh how nice." I say.

"Yeah," he says. "Some weekends I stop by if I have time." "Did you know we also have an RV Park here in Pine Mountain?"

I look up at him, "The one right down the road? I saw it coming in!"

"Yep, that's the one." he says. "Maybe one day you can bring your RV here and stay for a week."

"I might just do that." I say.

He grabs my hand and we cross the busy street to the other cute shops across the road.

"Be careful, this sidewalk is bumpy" he tells me as he squeezes my hand!

Carson smiles from ear to ear. His girl finally made it to his town! We walk behind a corner that is empty of people. I notice his eyes have a sparkle to them! My heart is racing a thousand miles a minute!

"I have to ask you something." He reaches his arm out for me "Come here". I move over to him and slide into his arms. His whole body is shaking. His fingers are shaking as he almost drops a tiny ring box with a heart on the front of it. He opens it up and reads this beautiful poem to me!

"~A Joy Forever~ A memory without blot or contamination must be an exquisite treasure, an inexhaustible source of pure refreshment. - Charlotte Bronte."

"Will you?" he asked me...

"Oh my gosh!" I scream. "Yes! Yes! Yes!" I hug him so tight and he leans down and kisses me!

"I want to be your best friend forever and never ever leave you!" he says "This is a Destiny Ring." he tells me, "This ring is very special to me, Please, don't ever lose it. It's the only one made like that in the world! I had a good friend custom make it! I have been waiting a long time for the right girl to come along. Geneva, you are the special girl I have been waiting for all my life."

"I really love it." I say.

He slides it on my finger and we emerge from behind the building!

"Would you like to meet one of my friends?" Carson asks me.

"Sure I would." I say.

We hurry across the busy downtown street, my ring sparkling in the sunlight. It almost lights up it's so shiny. My heart is racing from the wonderful surprise. We cross the crisscross patterned brick street and walk up to Gayla's Gift Shop. Carson still has hold of my hand.

"This is the place!" he says as he looks over at me.

Outside the store there is a display of art work from local artists and antiques from around the world.

Carson and I walk inside and are greeted his by friend Gayla. Inside the gift shop, I look up at the enormous ceiling. "This place used to be a bank." Carson says. I notice the many art pieces, beautiful clothing and hand crafted wood work.

Carson was chatting with Gayla as I came out of one of the rooms. I overhear Gayla say "Carson, she's cute!" I blush slightly. "What an amazing art shop you have" I tell her as I look over at Carson and he looks back at me. Gayla looks at us and smiles.

We say our goodbyes and exit the gift shop. The afternoon sun is shining brightly outside as Carson and I venture down the street to a Mexican restaurant. We walk the entire way.

I carefully pick up my Destiny Ring off of the table and examine its beauty.

"After 30 years, it still shines!" I say as tears well up in my eyes.

"He held my hand the whole way down to the Mexican Restaurant and he kept looking at the ring on my finger. Gladys! One time, he looked at it and winked at me!"

"What made him take you there?" Gladys asked me.

"Carson said it was a great place to eat lunch and it was!"

"Wow!" Gladys replied, "That is great."

"You missed some." I told her as I pointed to the napkin holder. "Under there." Gladys lifted the napkin holder and brushed the sugar granules out from underneath. "Now the table is clean." I tell her. Gladys laughs at me.

After we had lunch, we went to the Day Butterfly Conservatory at Callaway Gardens.

"I don't know what it is, Carson, but I'm reminded of butterflies all of a sudden!"

Carson laughs and says,

"That's the whole point, right?"

I laugh and say "Yes!"

He and I walk through the double doors leading out into the conservatory itself.

"It stays 70 degrees in here all year round and it's very humid!" he tells me as we enter the beautiful garden-like room!

The warm room is surrounded by glass windows and tropical vegetation. A butterfly lands on his shoulder. I look around and see thousands of blue butterflies fluttering and circling around us!

Citrus slices were placed under giant leaves. The butterflies have a place to rest and eat. The heavenly sounds of a waterfall and the laughter of Carson send a jolt of electricity through my heart.

We walk through another double glass door, past the cocoons and butterfly pictures to the gift shop.

We walk in and look at everything the butterfly gift shop has to offer! I bought a sheet of shiny stickers.

"Here, this is for you!" I say to Carson as I place a yellow 3d butterfly sticker on his shirt.

"Thanks." he says.

He smiles at me and pulls me in for a hug as we leave!

"I'll take you to a beautiful place." he says as he's backing out of the parking lot.

"Where's that?" I ask him.

"Lookout Point, it's just up the road!"

He drives about four miles and parks on the rock driveway overlook. The view is incredible! The air was clear. The smell of Brunswick stew and garlic bread from the Lookout restaurant saturates the air.

We stand gazing at the breathtaking view for a while. Then we drive across the street to the restaurant.

We walk into the stone restaurant at Lookout Point. Candies and gifts are displayed on every shelf. A wine room offers samples from local vineyards.

"Are you hungry? I am!" Carson says as we head toward the restaurant area in the back.

"How many"? The hostess asks.

"Just two." Carson answers

"Hold on just a minute." the hostess says as she leaves to look for a place.

It doesn't matter where we sit because every seat has a beautiful view. The large glass picture windows around the room give a perfect view of the valley.

We sit at a wooden table. On the table are brown paper placemats as well as silverware wrapped in light brown napkins. All of the brown tones give a rustic feel to the room. A large basket of fresh baked cheddar biscuits with butter is placed in front of us.

We ordered Brunswick stew and BLT sandwiches with French fries.

"That sounds so delicious, Geneva!" Gladys said.

"I know, Gladys" I say, as I wash our coffee mugs and place them on the shelf.

"We had a great talk about our future and our dreams." I say to Gladys.

I was going to get you a diamond ring, but that's the only one I could afford!" Carson says as he picks up his sandwich.

"That's ok, Carson." I say. "I love this ring. It's from your heart. Why would I want another one?"

Chapter Two

Sometimes I see him. Lately it's been almost every night. In one dream, he's walking up behind me in the store and I'm ordering a coconut cream cake with white icing. I know it is him, but I never turn around to look at him. I just know he is always a step behind me. Of course, I still have thoughts of him….in my dreams… … He always comes up and says he's sorry about everything. It's like nothing ever happened. We are still together, nothing changed, and I am the happiest girl on earth! In one dream, he walks up behind me and hugs me and I never want to wake up. I just want to stay there with him.

"That's exactly how I felt, Geneva when I lost my first boyfriend." Gladys is quick to answer as she is running her finger across the window seal of the doctor's office.

"Have I told you about the time he took me to Warm Springs?" I ask.

"No." Gladys replies.

"It was quite an interesting trip that day. It was March. The air from the winter made it cool. Carson invited me to go with him to the little town of Warm Springs."

 "Ever heard of it, Gladys?"

"It seems like I have, Geneva. Is it near Pine Mountain?"

"Yes it is! It's a very historical little town. Before we went over to Warm Springs, Carson has to stop by his friend Thomas' place.

I ride down to Thomas' house in Carson's truck. It is a long ride over the ridge. The trees are just waking up from winter.

 The rocks from the driveway make a funny sound under his wheels. Carson pulls up to the front door of a small house. Thomas is there to meet us on his front porch.

"What's up, man?" Thomas asked Carson

"Bringing her by man, what's up with you?"

Thomas never answers Carson. He just gives me a hard glare.

A dark cloud covers the valley out where we are and rain starts coming down. As we turn to go inside, Thomas says to me,

"You know, Geneva, my mom always told me this. When it rains, go put your ear to the ground and you can hear the sounds of hell underneath the dirt."

"Oh you didn't really do it, did you?" Gladys asked me with a shocked look on her face.

"No, I didn't actually do it. But, I'm sure he's done it a few times." I say. Gladys laughs.

We stay at Thomas' place about an hour. I get hungry, so we leave for Warm Springs.

There is a hamburger shop tucked behind quaint buildings. The smoke from the grill drifts through the trucks' open window.

"Here, this is for you!" Carson says. He reaches into his jacket pocket and hands me a beautiful dark crystal. "This is from the crystal mine in LaGrange. Keep it near you. It will protect you from bad dreams."

"Wow, that's beautiful." I say.

Driving through downtown Warm Springs, Carson parks his truck.

Old buildings line the main street of town. We walk up to a place called 'Eleanor's Alley'. We walk down the alley to a little hamburger shop.

The cool afternoon air sweeps across the table. We order one hamburger and one cheeseburger with no pickles!

"How do you feel about me?" Carson asks.

Stunned, I answer "Honestly?"

Carson answered "Yes."

I sit back in my chair and clear my throat a little as I smile. Birds flying over distract me from the sweet tea I am drinking.

"Honestly Carson, every time I see you, I'm reminded of a warm spring day. It's always spring when I'm with you. So if you really want to know, that's how I feel!"

Carson takes another bite of his hamburger.

"How do you feel?" I ask him.

"Well!" he answers, "You are very unique and unusual and… I don't think I've ever met someone quite like you before!"

I smile as my hand slides across the table, resting it on his. "And you wonder Carson, why I always call you my favorite guy?"

Carson smiles again. His eyes move downward do my hand to see his Destiny Ring sparkling in the sunshine.

After we eat lunch at the little grill, we walk around Warm Springs. We go into a little antique shop. All kinds of items ranging from Native American to 1950s retro are displayed.

"It seems like you two had a special bond." Gladys says as we are driving home. "We really did, Gladys… we really did!"

Gladys parks her car in a space close to her room at the retirement home.

"Dinner is being served. We better hurry in and get us a bite." she tells me as I walk in with her.

Sitting at the table, Gladys asks me

"So what happened after your trip to Warm Springs?"

 "I'll tell you about the time… it was in September, I saw him that September…, on a Saturday! He had the biggest smile on his face when he drove up! He gave me the biggest hug. Then he looked in my eyes for the longest and started laughing. It made me feel warm all over!"

"We jumped into his truck and went to Callaway Gardens."

Gladys smiles, "So what did the two of you do out there at the gardens?" she asks as I begin.

"Oh how beautiful!" I say as Carson and I walk toward the Discovery Center at Callaway Gardens.

The air out there has a crisp earthy smell to it. A calm wind brushes around the tops of the trees as he holds the door for me. We walk inside.

The Discovery Center is a large building with pine wooden rafters. The environment here is warm and friendly! This place houses a theater where you can watch a short movie about the gardens, a gift shop, a place for receptions and weddings and the Discovery Center café. That's where we ate!

"What was on the menu at the café?" Gladys asks me.

"Well, he got the BLT sandwich with potato chips and I got the chicken wrap with original sun chips and we both had sweet tea!"

"Yum." Gladys remarks. "What an interesting lunch."

"Yes it was! It was the best lunch I've had in years because he couldn't take his eyes off of me at all!"

Gladys giggles "He must've had it bad for you, girl!"

"He really did." I say. I kept telling him, "I think I'm dreaming." He had the biggest smile on his face all day!"

Gladys asks me "What did you two do after you ate?"

After we ate lunch together Carson asks,

"Would you like to walk to the chapel?"

"Yes, of course I would" I reply.

After all, we had the whole day to enjoy ourselves!

We walk across a long wooden bridge that crosses a small lake. He puts his arm around me and does not let go of me the whole time we are there! The grey paths lead us all the way to the chapel.

"Almost there." he tells me as my heart starts racing!

All of a sudden the whole garden gets quiet. He wraps his arms around me.

"Well, time for bed. I've got a big day tomorrow and I need to be 'chipper.' "Night, girl." Gladys interrupts.

"Goodnight Gladys." I reply.

I sit at the table remembering the visit to the chapel.

I hear the distant sounds of the chapel bell. I can smell the dirt and late blooming summer flowers. We walk down a grey foot path to the lovely chapel at Callaway Gardens!

"Let me show you the chapel" Carson says.

We walk into the chapel; its splendor takes my breath away. "Wow" I say.

The chapel is a beautiful tiny church with two enormous stained glass windows at either end. The pews are a beautiful light brown and the ceiling is arched in a gothic design. At the front of the church sits a tiny cross on a small table. We walk up to the cross and look at it for a while! Someone begins playing an old hymn on the chapel organ.

Carson tells me the chapel hosts many weddings and he would like it to host his someday.

"Beautiful"! I say to Carson.

"The bells start chiming again, marking the time. We sign the guest book.

"Enjoy your day" a sweet lady says as she holds the door for us. The heavenly music follows us outside.

"Wow!" I say again. "I have to be dreaming, Carson."

"Dreams aren't real." he replies.

I laugh and say, "I know I'm dreaming."

We follow a path behind the church. Grey rocks stand against pretty green foliage. A gentle stream trickles over the rocks, blending its music with the chapel bells.

"Say hello to the backyard rock garden! When I was a kid, I would play out here all the time!" he says as he runs and climbs on the rocks.

"Hah! There you are!" I say.

I take a picture of him on the rocks. A tiny stream trickles out of the rocks, making a musical sound. He reaches down and sifts through the sand with his fingers.

"Here, look. I call this a moon rock. It's native to this part of Georgia." he says, picking up a small rock.

I reach over and take the rock out of his wet hand covered in brown sparkly sand.

The golden September sky has suddenly turned eerily dark. As we walk back through Callaway Gardens, Carson looks up at the sky.

"We usually get strange weather here. I love lightning storms. Have I told you?"

"Well, I think you did once." I say.

"I just like the distant storms. I don't get in the bad ones."

All of a sudden, we feel rain drops. I look up, it is getting darker.

"Hold my hand." Carson says to me as we run down the grey path back to the Discovery Center.

By the time we make it to the Discovery Center, we are soaking wet. The air conditioner feels like ice on our wet clothes as we walk inside. I look down to see a pattern on the floor where rain water has dripped off of our wet clothing. It almost looks like the shape of a heart!

With the chicken wrap and rain soaked clothes, one of my first tastes of Pine Mountain is the sweetness of a best friend topped and diced with love.

Chapter Three

The storm blew in like nothing I've ever seen before. The rain was crashing against the window of my room. I close my eyes tightly and pull the two covers over my head to blot out the flashing lightning!

"Gladys… Gladys!" I holler but no one hears me.

The rain and occasional rumble of thunder continues into the night. I eventually drift off into a deep sleep.

"Ding." "Ding." The morning bell rings. Then, a friendly 'Happy Easter' greeting follows. It is morning and the storm is over. I notice Gladys is already up, getting ready to take me to her old house for Easter dinner.

"Good Morning, Gladys!" I say to her.

"Morning, Geneva. Are you about ready to go?" Gladys doesn't want to eat with all the others at the home today. Her kids are having a huge dinner and she never misses a chance with them.

I get up and get dressed. George stops by to wish us Happy Easter.

"I think my children will love you, Geneva." Gladys says.

"That brings me back, Gladys!" I reply. Gladys takes her three grocery bags and purse and places them on the chair by the door.

"I remember the time I made him laugh really hard! I remember he used to call me on his way home from work. We usually talked and laughed until he drove into his driveway! One time I got smart with him and he called me stubborn and a sassy cat! I said, 'Oh yes I am stubborn and sassy.' We were best friends. It felt good knowing there was always someone there when I needed him"! I say.

Gladys and I left and headed out to her car. The house she grew up in is a huge white three story Victorian home. The old house is across town in the historic district.

"My home has been in the family for years, Geneva!" Gladys says as she starts her car.

"This place, I hope, will remain in my family for many more years to come!" She says as I rest my head on the seat and smile at her. "What?" She asks me as she backs out of her space.

"Why does it always rain in my dreams, Gladys? I mean, there's always either a storm that brings these dreams on or in my dream it's raining?" I ask her.

"Maybe it was raining when you met him and you didn't even know it?" she says.

"It was summer, Gladys, and it was very hot when we met. I know… I was there!" I say.

"You know how I feel about dreams, Geneva. I don't believe they are real!" she says.

"I know Gladys, but when I close my eyes at night, they seem real!" I say.

Gladys doesn't say another word until we pull into the driveway of the huge three story house. I feel honored to have dinner with Gladys's family.

"Watch your step in the driveway. You may step in a sunken place!" Gladys warns.

I step out onto the white rock driveway and gaze up at the house. It is huge! Three stories! The windows in this house are small containing rippled glass and on the corners are lacy looking wooden carvings. The stairs on the front porch creak as Gladys and I carry the bags into the dining area. Her son and daughter- in- law have decorated their home for the Easter meal.

The dining table has a white tablecloth on the table. There are two vases of daffodils with white and yellow carnations and baby's breath. In the middle of the table are small baskets of colored eggs at each place.

Gladys introduces me to her son and daughter- in-law.

After the Easter blessing, we eat a scrumptious dinner consisting of ham, green beans, potato salad, candied yams and jello for dessert. Everyone devours the potato salad. It tastes like a baked potato.

After dinner, everyone goes into the living room to drink coffee and visit.. I grab a cup of coffee and make my way outside to try out one of the rocking chairs on the front porch. It is a pleasant day. The weather is comfortable and partly sunny.

As I sip my coffee, I lay my head on the rocker and close my eyes for a few minutes.

"Happy Easter, baby!" I say to him as I lean over and kiss his cheek! The dogwoods are blooming white in Pine Mountain and the sun seems to sparkle off them. It reminds me of snow.

"I love Callaway!" I say to Carson as we are riding through the gardens.

"I love being with you!" he says.

I lean up against his arm while the cool air blows against my face. It is a nice spring day and he has his windows down.

"I love you, my favorite guy!" I am quick to tell him before my dream starts fading.

I wake up with a slight headache from sitting in the sun on Gladys' old porch! Light laughter fills the living room as I open the screen and go inside.

Gladys and her kids are remembering good times.

"Geneva, where have you been?" Gladys asks.

"This old lady had to have a rest after that wonderful dinner!" I say back to her.

"How did you like the front porch?" her son David asks.

"Oh it was great." I say as I smile to myself.

I take my cup into the kitchen, following Margaret.

"Can I help you?" I ask.

"Sure." Margaret says.

She and I wash the dishes left over from dinner.

Evening finally arrives. I look around to find Gladys gathering some of the food left over from lunch today.

"Geneva, would you like some of this jello?" she asks as she spoons food into take-home dishes.

"Sure I would!" I say.

There is a slice of chocolate cake on a plate with two forks.

"Ha!" I laugh to myself.

"What, Geneva?" Gladys asks.

"That piece of chocolate cake sitting over there reminds me of the time Carson and I went to the Burger Place in Pine Mountain. After he and I had a hamburger, he ordered a piece of chocolate lava cake. The server brought it out with two forks neatly placed on the little dish. What a nice memory!"

Gladys looks down at the leftover dishes and smiles while she loads what she wants into her containers.

"We won't have to eat in the cafeteria this evening. Sometimes I get tired of the food at the home." Gladys says.

"I agree" I say. She and I take dishes of food and two vases of daffodils out to her car.

David and Margaret invite us to have one last treat before we leave. Margaret has baked a special Easter bread.

Gladys starts to cry as she tells her children goodbye! After hugs and well wishes, Gladys and I are on our way back to the home.

"Geneva, what did you dream about on the front porch today?" asks Gladys.

I leaned my head back and smile as we pass through an intersection.

"I was at Callaway Gardens with Carson."

"I knew it! I knew it!" Gladys laughs as she nods her head.

She turns on her radio and starts singing to a country song.

"Gladys, you're funny!" I say as she speeds up. "We need to get out more often!"

"Right we do!" she says back to me.

Pulling into the lot at the home, Gladys parks her car in her regular space.

That evening, Gladys and I chow down on leftovers from lunch.

"His eyes… I loved his eyes!" I tell her as she and I eat.

I feel happy going to bed that night. The storm from early this morning fades into the back of my mind. I close my eyes…

It was only late summer. Gentle rain drops fall softly around me as I stand outside Carson's truck. I am holding his hand with both of mine, feeling its coarseness and tracing the lines of his palm before leaning my forehead down on his knuckles. I am laughing so hard. I keep laughing until I look up and see his face.

"I wish you lived here!" he says.

"I will soon, I hope!" I say.

The sun comes out all of a sudden in Pine Mountain, making the drops of rain look like drops of gold falling out of the sky.

"I love you!" Carson says.

Chapter Four

"Gladys, did I tell you about the time he and I went to a powwow?"

"No, you didn't! Tell me about it!" Gladys says as she looks through papers on her tiny desk.

"This was the annual Mother's Day Powwow and it was held every year at a park in North Georgia" I say to Gladys as I start to remember.

"Did I ever tell you, Geneva, my mother always called me Gladiola"? Gladys says.

"That's pretty, Gladys." I say as I smile.

"Yes, when she would call me, she would say 'Gladiola! Where are you'?"

I laugh as she and I walk to the home's library. I remember it now…

Carson and I drove to the powwow.

"I wish I could walk you through my heart." I say to him.

The road to the event area is rain soaked. The smell of wood smoke and fry bread saturates the air as we look for a place to park. We find a place underneath the trees in the grass.

My heart is filled with excitement! "I can't wait to get inside!" I tell Carson.

After paying, we enter through the gate crossing Etowah River. There are tents lined up in a semi-circle around the park. Smoke is billowing out of one of the tents.

"That must be the hamburger shop!" I say.

We make our way to the dance area where the grand entry is about to begin. The dancers are dressed in fringe and bells. Some of them carry sticks and feather staffs into the dance circle.

"Hold my hand" Carson says.

I grab his hand tightly. A prayer is said in English and Cherokee as total silence drifts over the crowd.

"Hold on to me" Carson says.

The singing starts followed by drumming! I take Carson's arm and we enter the dance circle.

"Boom" "boom" "boom!"

The drum makes a haunting sound across the hills of North Georgia! Many people are sitting around the dance circle. Some are just watching the grand entry; some taking pictures.

My sweaty hands caused my ring to slide to the tip of my finger and I almost lose it. At the end of the dance circle, a long line has formed for everyone to honor the veterans. We do.

"Oh to go back to that day, Gladys!" I say as I take a book off a shelf of the small library.

"I found one!" Gladys says.

"Found what?" I ask her.

"I found a copy of that book I've wanted to read for the longest and yay, I finally have a copy!" She blows the dust off of the old book.

"So, Geneva," she says, "Tell me more about the powwow."

I close my eyes again.

"It's about to rain!" I tell him as we run into the nearest tent.

The rain seems to taper off into a steady drizzle! A woman is getting ready to sing on the stage. The rain picks up and gets harder and louder as it pours down. She begins to sing and the rain suddenly stops.

"Wait, Geneva, you mean the rain just stopped and it got sunny?" Gladys asked.

"No, Gladys. While she was singing, the rain quit falling. It was like God stopped to listen to the hauntingly beautiful melody. There was total silence and everyone turned to listen. It was amazing!"

After the singing, we ate warm fry bread and had our picture taken in front of a tipi!

"And all I have to do is close my eyes, Gladys, and I can still smell the fry bread cooking!" I say.

"He treasured the photo from the photographer's camera. I did too because it was so beautiful!" I say.

"At least you remember the good times you had!" Gladys says.

"I do, Gladys… I really do!" I say.

I went to bed that night tossing and turning. Tomorrow is Mother's day at the home. I am afraid to close my eyes but I eventually do… fading into another realistic dream…I am stirring a cup of warm soup, held by my chapped hands. The spoon clicks against the white glass cup making a funny jingle sound. He is standing right there in front of me smiling.

"I!"… I begin to tell him. January's blues must've sunken into me. He is trying to cheer me up.

"Don't cry". Tears are flowing down my cheeks.

"Please don't cry" he tells me again as he gently wipes tears from my face.

"I wish I could see you again." I say. "I wish this wasn't just a dream!"

Carson continues to wipe my tears away. Only one tear falls into the soup making a heart shape with swirls around it.

"Don't you feel better now?" Carson asks me.

"I always feel good when you're around." I tell him.

He reaches out and hugs me, propping his chin gently on the top of my head.

Then the morning bell rings. Gladys and I skip breakfast but go down to eat lunch. It is really special today.

Pink and white roses adorn the lunch tables. On the menu is steak, green beans, mashed potatoes with gravy, yams, collard greens and your choice of a roll or cornbread. For dessert it's a choice of key lime pie, coconut cream pie or Boston crème pie. All of these items are selected by the nursing home director. They are specially selected out of the personal recipe book from her mother.

"I hate days like this." Gladys says.

"We eat. Then our kids come to see us. Then it's time for bed. Nothing ever happens here!" she tells me as we sit to be served.

"I know, Gladys" I say. "I wish my mother would come walking in right now!"

Not a single one of us speaks at the dinner table. Holidays like this are always quiet, solemn, and sometimes a little sad.

A blessing is said by the resident pastor. Then the director stands and speaks. She honors all moms both past and present. She talks about her memories growing up. There is much laughter and some tears. Dinner is delicious. It reminded me of my mom's cooking.

Days like this are hard, but we get through it. I remember to bring my beaded pouch with my Destiny Ring inside. I slide two fingers inside the soft warm pouch to find its comfort. I slide the ring onto my index finger, feeling the cool silver against my skin. Then with my other finger I find the teardrop aquamarine which is very cold to the touch. Gladys looks over at me with my pouch in my lap.

"He told me not cry today, so I won't, Gladys!" I tell her.

Gladys smiles as she is eating. After dessert, we leave the lunch room and head back to our rooms.

Gladys and I are always last to leave. We like to visit with a few of our friends.

As we walk down the hall to our rooms, the lingering aroma of steak and candied yams follow closely behind us. The smell reminds me of the time I ate at a steak and hamburger place in Pine Mountain. It is sunset and Carson and I are sitting on the outdoor dining porch. It is the most beautiful place. Looking out across the hills seems like looking into forever.

Gladys sits still, nervously tapping her foot.

Gladys and I had a very long and tiring day. Gladys taps her foot when she is remembering. I just get quiet and sit still when I remember!

I wake up to see Gladys asleep in her chair.

I pull myself up out of my chair. I take my brown pouch and put it up against my heart, walking up to the window of my room. The evening sky is streaked with purple and orange, fading with memories from today and making room for a new day filled with joy in the morning.

What a day it has been I think to myself. What a day it has been.

Chapter Five

"The light in Pine Mountain seems different. It brings an atmosphere of vacation and a new adventure!" I say as Gladys and I walk through the flower garden of the home.

The home's garden is beautiful. It has all kinds of plants and herbs. There is even a small vegetable garden up against the brick wall. Gladys and I bring our gardening gear. We take our places on the cool cement in the shade of the giant tree in the middle of the garden.

"So what's on your mind, Geneva?" Gladys asked.

"I'm just remembering that terrible day in June." I say. "He didn't choose me. I chose to move on. I lost touch with him after that day. I thought if he made his choice on someone else, then it's his loss. He made that choice, not me. What more can I say, Gladys?"

"You need to quit dwelling, girl!" Gladys tells me as she sifts through the soft dirt in the rose garden.

"It has been thirty years but now I'm thinking of him every day!" I say.

Gladys takes her things and pushes herself up off of her gardening pillow half covered in black potting soil and red Georgia dirt. She brushes the dirt off her jeans.

"Well, I've got to go grab me something cold. Want to come along? You'll feel a lot better if you have a drink in you!" She says.

"Sure, I'll come along with you!" I say. Iced tea is delicious on a warm day in May.

I sit there at the table looking at the garden, wondering… Why am I thinking about him?

That night I have a strange dream. I am standing on a rock in solid darkness; I look around me… nothing.. All of a sudden I look around me and see something flashy in the distance. I can't make out what it is until I hear the ringing of it through the air.. It's the ring and it's flying towards me at 90 miles an hour … All of a sudden a hand reaches out to catch it. It's Carson!

"You really thought your ring would hit you in the face?" He says to me through the night.

"I thought it would, Carson."

"Look on your hand" he says.

All of a sudden I look down and there it is on my hand!

"How did it get there?" I ask him.

I look up and he is gone! I look on my hand and there are two rings! One of them is my Destiny Ring!

"That was a strange dream, Gladys." I say as I trace the top of my cup with my fingers. "Maybe it was something I ate for dinner last night that caused me to have such a strange dream!"

Gladys turns around to face me "Maybe it's the fact that YOU never gave up on him." she says.

"I never did, really. I had to go on with my life without him. I was told a long time ago to trust your heart!" I say.

"Well, what DOES your heart tell you now, Geneva?" Gladys asked.

"My heart tells me that one day I will see him again. I'm an old woman now. If I were to run into him, do you think he'll recognize me at all?" I ask.

"Geneva" Gladys says as she sits down beside me.

"Geneva, I had a friend once that I lost touch with for fifteen years!"

"My friend NEVER forgot about me. When I saw that friend again, even after fifteen years it was if we had never been apart. That is how friends are with each other. Now, I have to go, I hope you feel better, girl!"

I smile. "See you, Gladys, have a great day!" I tell her as she is leaving.

I lean my head back against the wall of the garden and smile to myself thinking of what she said. I fall asleep.

The lunch bell wakes me. My heart starts racing. It was a good dream. I try to remember it the whole way down to the lunch room.

I get my tray of food and sit beside Gladys.

"Are you all right, girl?" Gladys asked me.

"I'm fine!" I say "I just had another dream."

"Well" Gladys said "What was it about exactly? Do tell me?" Gladys says with a smile.

It was his birthday. I met him at the beach at Callaway Gardens so we could swim. The white sand of the beach met my toes. The warm breeze of summer blows my hair around; The West Georgia air is warm and inviting. Waiting for him, I walk down the long beach.

"So did he ever show?" Gladys asked.

"He did eventually show up!" I say, as I take another bite of food.

"He told me he would meet me under the pavilion at the beach area!" I say, as Gladys smiles at me.

"He is wearing bright red swim trunks and a big smile. He comes up and hugs me like he hasn't seen me in years.

He puts his arm around me and walks me over to the concessions to buy drinks for us.

"So he treated you to a drink?" Gladys asks me.

"Yes he did!" I say "He was sweet like that!"

He and I walk over to the giant chess set where a few folks are playing on the board.

There is a giant chair you can sit in to have your picture made. It is a huge Adirondack white chair and there is a line for pictures. We have our picture made in the chair, and then swim out to an inflatable called Aqua Island. We have so much fun!

All of a sudden, the bell rings in the home "Ding!" "Ding!" A frantic voice comes over the speaker.

"Residents, make your way into the hallway in the middle of the building! We are under a tornado warning! Please, make your way to the nearest hallway!"

Gladys looks around as people are hastily getting up out of chairs and moving into the hallway.

"I thought it was sunny outside." Gladys says.

"Me too." I say.

"When did this come up?" I ask.

The nurses, along with the director and the secretary from the front office, are on hand to get everyone escorted into the nearest hallway. Two nurses bring chairs in from the lunch room so some residents will have a seat.

I see George. He makes the whole situation a joke. I see him making two nurses laugh. He is like that.

Gladys and I are crammed about halfway down the hallway. It seems like thousands of people are in line waiting on a celebrity to arrive, but that isn't the case. I leave Gladys, squeezing my way through the people, slowly making my way down the hallway to look outside.

It is ugly. It looks just like night outside. The wind is blowing and I see a few balls of hail blow inside. The two front sliding doors are propped open.

"Geneva! Geneva, wake up! The storm is over!" The director finds me in a chair by the front door. I fell asleep again and didn't know it.

"Is the storm over?" I ask her.

"Yes it's over. You may return to your lunch. If you would like it heated, just let one of the servers know!"

"Ok" I say, as I lift myself up out of the chair.

I find Gladys back in the lunchroom chatting with one of her friends about the bad storm. Her friend is discussing a story of a tornado they had in Oklahoma.

"Geneva, your lunch got cold on you!" Gladys says.

"Oh I know. I fell asleep again. The director woke me up and reminded me!" I say as I smile.

I take my seat at the table.

"So, Geneva, you were telling me about the beach experience you had with Carson? Tell me, did you two go swimming?" she asked.

"We sure did" I say. I stop suddenly.

"What is it?" Gladys asked.

 I put my napkin up to my face.

 "What?" Gladys asked again as her friend glances over at me.

"Have you ever had a memory you never wanted to leave?" I asked.

"We all have those, girl" Gladys says.

.

"After we took a splash in the lake, he took me to a little restaurant beside Chipley Corners in Pine Mountain."

"Oh nice" Gladys says.

"We walk in and everyone is there- his friends and his family. This is his birthday surprise!"

I wipe my face again with my napkin.

"His cake is an amazing work of art. Chocolate with two candles on it- a two and a five!"

"Wow" Gladys says as she gets up to go back to her room. "That sounds like he had a wonderful birthday."

"It's one of my most treasured memories! I remember the look on his face! What a surprise to see his folks there! He got teary eyed!"

After lunch, I decide to go back to my room and relax a little. Down the hall is a tall mirror. Gladys always tells me that all mirrors reflect the truth, even when you don't want to see it. The truth is always there!

I glance into the mirror only for a split second. I see someone standing right behind me in the reflection. It is Carson! I turn around to look but there is no one behind me. I guess Gladys is right mirrors reflect truth. This mirror reflected something true- what's in my heart!

Chapter Six

Of course, I always cried when I left Pine Mountain. I never wanted to leave. That was just my nature.

"I remember that evening, Gladys. It was late fall. It was sunset. The sky was a soft pink color and the clouds were a deep purple.

A soft breeze blows through my hair. The trees around me are whispering their evening song. Birds are landing in the field, grazing on an evening meal over conversation with each other before nightfall.

My ring fits snugly on my finger giving off a blueish purple tint against the sky. I walk over to a patch of rocks and pick up a piece of flint rock before returning to my car.

"That's a wonderful memory"! Gladys says as she makes her way into the auditorium to have a seat.

"I was there for a second, Gladys"! I say as I take my seat right beside her.

The sun is setting over the town this evening. My mind drifts away into a place far in the corners of my memories.

"I was thinking about Carson and the walk we took in October. It was where he loves to go and I was glad I was with him." I say.

"What did you two do out there? Huh?" Gladys nudges my ribs as we sit and wait for the monthly meeting at the home.

I quietly sit back in my chair and smile.

"Well, I won't tell you everything we did." I laughed, "We just took a walk!"

Gladys looks over at me again, raising her eyebrows.

"Really, Gladys, that's all we did." I say, smiling.

I close my eyes for a few seconds. I hate monthly meetings at the home. By the time the speaker gets up to speak, I am walking with my best friend on a warm October day, down a wooded path.

As we walk through the woods, we pass a small trickling stream. He finds a piece of aquamarine almost shaped like the one in the Destiny Ring. I take it and place it in my leather pouch so I won't lose it.

We walk up a tall hill and back down and out of the wooded area into a large field where our cars are parked.

We forget the time. Carson has to go and so do I. Getting through Atlanta will take some time with all the traffic.

"Give me a hug" Carson says.

I lean over and hug him tight.

Tears are welling up in my eyes, just like they always do when I have to leave him.

"Don't worry. There will be other times." he says.

"I'll be back!" I smile at him and say "Bye, baby!"

He closes his truck door and drives off. I am right behind him, teary eyed.

"Bye best friend" I whisper to myself as I drive off,

"Geneva…. Geneva…. Hey Geneva" Gladys nudges me. "The meeting is over, wake up!"

I open my eyes to see that the meeting is over. Everyone is leaving the room.

"You fell asleep, girl" Gladys tells me.

"I know" I say "It was a wonderful dream!"

I get up out of my chair and follow Gladys into the refreshment area. We each take a cup of juice and a plate of cookies and walk down to the activity room.

"So what did you dream about this time, Geneva?" Gladys asks me.

"It was October. I was with him."

Gladys takes a sip of juice

"He and I were walking in the woods" I tell her.

"Well, that sounds like a nice dream" Gladys said as she smiles.

The next morning, a loud noise wakes me up. I get up and dress for the day. Walking into the breakfast room downstairs, I notice Gladys isn't there. Her coffee cup is untouched. I walk up to the front desk and ask "Where is Gladys?" They tell me she went out on an early trip with the group. I walk back to the breakfast table to eat and drink coffee… alone this morning!

The silence in the room gives way to the sound of a ticking clock… tic…tic…tic… My mind seems to wander as I close my eyes. I am heading to Columbus to perform in a show. I was a country music singer back then and I invited him to go with me.

"What kind of music will you be performing?" he asks me.

"Country, of course" I say.

The road whined below us, making a steady beat like a drum.

"We're here!" I smile.

He brought his guitar and accompanied me on a couple of songs.

We end the performance with a group song. The audience loves us!

"I've never had so much fun in my life"! Carson says as we are leaving.

The drive home is beautiful. I have my hair down, blowing in the breeze.

"I love you." he looks over at me and says.

"I love you too, Carson. We had fun tonight!" I say back.

We finally make it back to Pine Mountain. The most beautiful song starts playing on the radio as we pull into the lighted parking lot of the Chipley Corners. I get out of my car only to find him meeting me on the other side. He takes me into his arms, brushes my hair back and kisses me on the forehead.

"I really had fun tonight!" he told me again in a soft voice.

"Me too" I whisper as he holds me tightly in his arms.

I open my eyes to a cold breakfast and lukewarm coffee. Gladys was sitting across the table from me.

"How long have you been sitting there?" I ask her.

"Forever" she says. "I thought you were never going to wake up, girl."

"I didn't really want to this time, Gladys. I loved the dream I was in" I say as I smile.

Gladys has put her box of sugar on the counter, along with napkins and a few items needed for the breakfast room.

"You know when I dream, Geneva, I never remember them. It's useless to dwell on it. That's what my mother always told me growing up."

The lunch bell rings. It has been a long morning and I am starved.

"I hope it's not lima beans for lunch again!" Gladys says as we walk to the lunch room.

"Yeah, me too" I say.

Gladys is happy. No lima beans on the menu today! Green peas were sitting beside bright orange carrots. I sit down tearing off the paper from the straw beside my glass of tea.

"We used to take them and blow the paper off at each other!" Gladys says as she crumples up someone's left over paper sitting on the table. "Like this" she says as she blows the paper from her straw across the table.

After lunch, Gladys sits with me for a while, talking about her kids and her house.

"My true love blessed me with two beautiful kids!" she says smiling.

"Did I tell you what I said to him, Gladys?" I say.

She stops and looks over at me.

"No, said what to him?" she answered.

I look down at my ring which is in my palm, rolling around and flashing it's brightness in the light.

"I told him that I thank God every single day that I have a friend like him!" I say.

I clutched my ring tightly and smile. I always called him 'baby'. I only knew one other friend who called her husband "baby" and that was Gladys! I guess you could say that's why we were like sisters, both of our favorite guys were named "baby".

Lunch was amazing! Gladys and I laughed over remembered good times and our true loves. I reflected on the life I've lived and how it bloomed into a beautiful family. Later its petals left me here, leaving me only to remember. Neither time nor distance will keep me locked away from Pine Mountain and the guy I knew there. All I have to do is close my eyes.

Mid - summer seemed to fade into deep fall and the leaves swirl around the black top parking lot in a whirlwind. Halloween was tomorrow and the director of the home assigned everyone a job to do as an activity for the party. Gladys and I were in charge of making orange paper jack-o-lanterns.

"Oh, Geneva, we used to have the best Halloweens growing up." Gladys says.

I stop cutting out the eyes of a pumpkin and set my scissors down. Gladys looks over at me.

"What's wrong, Geneva?"

"It's Halloween" I say, "That was his favorite holiday!"

Gladys quickly takes a bite of cookie and turns toward me in her chair.

"What did you and he do at Halloween? Tell me!"

"He gave me the idea to dress as a cat. I went to children's hospitals and entertained children as a cat."

Gladys smiles at me. "That was a nice thing" she says.

"It was, and I'll never forget him for that inspiration." I sit back as I close my eyes again.

The sun is setting behind the small hill at the home and its rays have reached the orange cup sitting on the table, making it light up. I remember standing in his kitchen helping him carve a pumpkin.

"He was drinking out of his fear world cup" I tell her. It was orange and the eyes on the monster lit up in an eerie orange color and it would glow in the dark.

Gladys took another bite of her cookie and a sip from her green soda.

"Did both of you go out dressed in costume that night?" she asked.

"We did" I said to her. "He was a super hero and I was the cat."

"Interesting combination" Gladys says.

"We went downtown to stand in front of Gayla's Gift Shop and hand out candy to the kids!"

"What a wonderful Halloween we had, Gladys!" I say as I hand the pumpkin decorations to the home director.

The day had finally come to an end and I was very tired. I was quick to tell Gladys

"Goodnight" like I always do before I head to bed and drift off to sleep.

Chapter Seven

The rain gives me chills… I have hold of his hand, walking with him, soaking wet.. That's what I see after I crash. I have tears in my eyes and don't see the other car heading in the wrong direction toward me.

"I hope I mean so much to you" I say to him.

We are walking down a train trestle in the pouring rain. Just like he always does, he spins me around. He is about to answer me when I see a big bright light!

I wake up in the hospital with a huge gash. Bandages are wrapped around my head and I lay still in the bed. I can barely see the nurse leaning over me, calling me "sweetie" with every other word she says.

"Where is my ring?" I ask her

"Honey, you need to keep still" she answers.

"NO! WHERE IS MY RING??" I shout.

My belongings are in a clear plastic bag over on the shelf.

"Ouch" I shout.

"Honey, I told you, you need to keep still!" the nurse says out of frustration.

It was a cold November morning and I just woke up from a nightmare car crash.

I notice the clock in the room says 7:30 am and my whole body is numb. I look over and see all sorts of lead wires and monitors hooked up to me like I am a machine charging for tomorrow's use.

"After the doctor checks you out, you'll be discharged" the nurse tells me.

"Am I going to be ok? Do I have any broken bones?!" I ask her.

No broken bones, just a nasty cut!" the nurse says as she unravels the bandages on my head.

"The doctor should be in shortly to take a look at your cut."

"Was there any glass in it?" I ask her.

"No, we removed all of it There's no more glass." the nurse says.

"The doctor should be in shortly" she tells me again as she leaves the cold room.

The gentle hum of the air system voided the silence of the tiny hospital room as my friend gets up to check my gash.

"Gosh" she says in disbelief.

"Does it look bad?" I ask her.

"Not bad" she replies "It's already healing!" She says to me, bringing much needed relief to my anxiety.

"Can you get my ring? I want to hold it in my hands!" I ask.

This ring always brings me comfort. She reaches over and grabs it out of the bag full of my things and hands it to me.

It was still beautiful. Even after being knocked through a glass window and landing on hot pavement, then sliding into a flash flood of radiator fluid, I realized, the aquamarine jewel was untouched. She removed the ring from the bag and wiped it off with rubbing alcohol using a paper towel. I clutched the ring tightly in my right hand, and then I clutched it tightly with both hands.

 A knock at the door startles me.

"Come in" I say. It is the doctor and I hope he has good news.

His gaze is cold and his hands are firm. He has no idea I have the ring in my hand.

"Limit your activity for two weeks. No caffeine while you're on pain killers. If you get dizzy, lie down for 30 minutes. If condition worsens, come back." he says.

He looks at my stitched wound and lets out a sigh before he says,

 "The nurse will be in with your discharge papers." he leaves the room.

After about thirty minutes, the discharge nurse rolls in a wheelchair with another nurse right behind her.

"You are free to go, sweetie" she tells me as she's disconnecting the many wires hanging off me

The nurse helps me into the wheelchair and lays a cover over my legs to keep me warm. I close my eyes after that. I am exhausted. My ring rides in my right hand the whole way out.

"Oh my"! Gladys says as she was putting her shoes on. "It's a wonder you weren't killed."

"I know it, Gladys. I think what saved me was being with him after I closed my eyes that afternoon."

"Is that so? Do you really think that's what saved you?" Gladys asks.

"I think so" I say.

Gladys carefully pulls her suit jacket over her shoulders, making it look straight.

"Well, time to go girl. I have to go catch the show!" Gladys told me as she closes the door of the vanity.

November's chill reminds me of that terrible day.

"See ya later, girl!" Gladys says to me as she makes her way to the door.

"Later!" I say back to her.

I don't go to this evening's show. I am not interested.

I make my way down the hall to the tiny breakfast room to get my evening coffee. No one is sitting in the room, so I take my coffee and walk down the hall to the front atrium and the enormous stairs. I walk over and sit on the bottom step just gazing out the windows of the double sliding doors. It is evening in the home and everyone is either gone to the show or in their rooms fast asleep- except for me.

I lean my head against the bannister of the staircase and slowly sip my coffee when a noise comes from the director's office. It raises a memory in my mind that I had once wanted to forget forever.....

"Remember me, Carson! Promise me you'll remember me!..."

Those were the last words I said to him that November before he closed the door of his truck. Thomas was standing right beside me laughing his head off, making it look like I had done something wrong.

"Carson has already made his choice" Thomas snickers.

"REMEMBER ME!" I cry! "I LOVE YOU, CARSON!" I cry again, as I half follow him backing out of the downtown gas station parking lot in Pine Mountain.

Carson backs into five small shrubs, making a brushing sound and speeds off. After that, Thomas leaves in a hurry, trying to catch up with Carson. Thomas claims Carson was seeing another girl. But I never accepted the fact that he "loved" or was "in love" with her because I knew a secret… one I kept… He fell madly in love with a girl all right… but it was ME!

"Miss"…. "Miss?" Are you ok? The cleaning lady touches my shoulder.

I have fallen asleep on the stairs and didn't know it.

"I'm ok, I just fell asleep" I say.

"Just checking on you" she says with a smile.

I get up and take my cup down to the coffee room, wash it out and head back down the hallway to my room. It is a ghost town this evening. Only one person lingers by the door of a room, talking with a friend.

I walk to my room and close the door. I feel chilly so I take a quick wash off and go to bed early… in a raging fever…

"Ding" "Ding" The morning bell forces my heavy eyes open. I sit up, slowly wiping my eyes. I walk to the sink and wash my face. This sore throat I have makes my knees feel painful and difficult to move.

I slowly make my way down to the breakfast room where I find Gladys reading a newspaper!

"Did you live through last night?" she asks me.

"Yeah, Gladys, I did!" I say as I get my cup down from the counter.

"But I thought I wasn't going to" I say to her.

"I don't usually give in to a sore throat" I say again as I reach for a doughnut

"Well, you're coming back to the land of the living!" Gladys says as she turns a page of the paper.

I quietly sit at the table, leaning my head up against the wall.

"What are you thinking of?" Gladys asks.

"The time I told him to keep me locked in his heart forever and don't let anyone ever take me out." "You know, Gladys, I still feel him in my heart somewhere. I've kept him in a very special place!"

"I'll remind you again, girl, how many YEARS ago was that?" she asked me.

I take another bite of my doughnut and let it slowly slide down my sore throat. Then I mix the doughnut with warm coffee.

"I remember when I told him that, Gladys. Keep me locked in your heart and never let me out!"

Gladys folds her paper closed and places it on the table. She looks up and says,

"When did you tell him this?"

"On a day he and I went for a walk. It was overcast that day." I answer.

"Carson, listen to me. Listen!" I say as I stop him in his tracks. "I'm always here for you."
I say.

"I know, but something's on my mind" he says.

We start walking down the sidewalk, eventually making our way to the back of a church in downtown Pine Mountain.

"What will happen if we lose touch?" he asks me.

"Why would you think we'll lose touch, Carson?" I ask.

"Well, just stuff going on right now. It's wearing me down so bad!"

He never told me what troubled him that day. Later, I did find out. It was this other girl.

"I want you to remember something, ok?" I tell him.

"Sure" he says.

"Lean down" I whisper.

.He leans down and I kiss the crease where his forehead met his nose.

"Keep me locked in your heart and never ever let anyone take me out of it, you hear me?" I whisper.

"I promise, Geneva! You are in my heart forever. You have my ring right?" he asks.

36.

"Of course I do! I will keep it forever!" I say.

He smiles softly and kisses the top of my head.

We walk down the sidewalk back to our cars parked in front of the bank.

"Carson opens the door to his truck, Gladys, and turns his radio on really loud!" I laugh as I remember.

"He did?" Gladys asks.

"Yes! I remember it was swing music, the kind we love dancing to!"

"He took my hands and we dance on the brick sidewalk that evening!" I say, smiling.

Gladys wrinkles her forehead again.

"That's sweet!" she says.

"I hated to leave!"

"I can understand why!" Gladys replies.

I told him bye and hugged him tightly. I got teary eyed before leaving. It was kind of a tradition to cry, I guess.

Gladys looks over at me again.

"Remembering and going back in your mind can be viewed as an illness!" Gladys says. She laughs and says "Scared ya!"

Fall's light dimly fades into a pink sunset with streaks of yellow and swirls of orange giving summons of winter's arrival. My memories keep coming back- whether in my dreams or merely just a thought running across my mind. It could be the dawn of a new day in the spring when first light barley touches the tops of the trees when I think of him. Or, it could be in the solid stillness of winter when frost on grassy hills sparkles in the light like thousands of diamonds.

But, in love, there is no season.

I think of this as I look outward through the window of the home.

I will forever be left in the wonder of why? I always yearn to go back to those sun -filled days when there was no worry.

But in truth, my life had a plan to follow a path of new love and a family.

Always in my heart, I believed Carson was my Destiny.

I never shared my secret with anyone else until lately. The memories haunt me. I need an answer or maybe conquer my fear of continual wonder.

I see some new folks walking with the director of the home. Gladys is gone again.

I do something different today. I sit at a lace covered table in front of a picture window. I am looking out at our garden. Birds are flying around the feeder outside, eating the seed.

It's a quiet morning so far.

A memory suddenly flashes across my mind.

I'm holding a bottle in my hand. Carson and I drive up to the ridge in Pine Mountain.

"This root beer is delicious!" I say.

Yeah, but it tastes more like licorice to me." Carson replies, taking a sip of his root beer.

On the ridge, there is a small trail leading down to a tree where ten crosses are placed in a neat row.

"What's down there? "I ask.

"Those are the markers of teenagers who drove too fast around the corner and ended up down there." Carson says.

"Oh, that's terrible! "I say.

"That's right." Carson says.

He stops and picks up a glass bottle and throws it down the hill...

WHAM! A sound startles me and I open my eyes.

"Wake up! George says, knocking his cane on the table.

"You scared me!" I say with a fearful look on my face.

"You were asleep!" George replies.

"I better pour my coffee out. It's cold!" I say. "How are you anyway, George? Did you hear from your daughter?"

"Not yet! She's still on business!" he says.

"If you hear from her, tell her I said 'best wishes'!" I say.

"I will, Geneva, have a great day!" he replies.

I smile at him as he makes his way to the lunch room. The usual morning social is taking place amongst the men of the home.

I try not to close my eyes again for fear of a memory returning. Maybe I should reminisce on better times. When I remember Pine Mountain, it's like I'm really there.

I remember the way his truck smelled. I think of the great fun we had when we were together. His friendship brought me happiness.

The need to know what happened to Carson soaks through me.

It's that time of year when I feel this way. When summer leaves and the warmth outside turns cool.

It was summer when I saw him last, thirty years ago. I am truly blessed to have such wonderful memories of Pine Mountain and of a dear friend. These memories now live in my heart in a very special place.

Chapter Eight

"Remember that day after work, Carson? I came to see you and you were upset about something?" I say.

"Yep, sure do. You made me feel a lot better too!" he answers.

"Yes, it made my heart smile, because I made you smile" I say.

"My memories never fade, Gladys" I say as I wipe my nose.

"My looks can fade, but my memories...well, never!"

"Geneva, I think I'll get ready to go to the grocery store!" Gladys says.

"Hey, I'll go with you!" I say.

Gladys has to get a few things for tonight's ice cream social. We get to pick out a few ice cream flavors and get some sodas and specialty finger food. We volunteered to shop for the event and we get to choose our favorites!

"Are you ok, Geneva?" Gladys asks me as we drive to the store.

"I'm fine" I say.

I forgot my leather pouch and left it sitting on the breakfast room table. Forgetting it made me feel a little incomplete and disconnected in some way.

"Really, Geneva, are you ok?" Gladys asks again.

"Gladys, seriously, I'm fine!" I say as sweat drops form on my forehead. "I just forgot my ring!"

"Oh" Gladys replies. "We won't be gone long, you know!" she says.

All of a sudden, a giant red wasp flies into Gladys windshield, making a loud pop sound as Gladys taps her brake and says,

"What was that?"

I look over at her and reply, "A wasp."

"That was quite loud!" she says.

I smile! The thought of a wasp suddenly gets me to thinking

"He walked me past a large tree one time. I had no idea what he was doing. He leaned down, picked something up, and put it behind his back."

"What was it? A surprise?" Gladys asks me.

"Better. It was a wasps' nest! It was empty, of course!" I say.

"I found you something! It's all I can give you today for a memory." Carson says.

"Something you might be able to use in your art!" I look up at him "Oh really?" I say.

"Yes, here!" Carson pulls out this beautiful giant wasp nest.

"Wow, I've never seen one that big before in my life!" I say as he smiles.

"Keep it dry so it doesn't break apart." he tells me, as he hands it over to me.

I hold it in my left hand. My ring sparkles as I walk back to my car with him to say bye for the evening.

"We're here!" Gladys says as she's parking in the handicapped space at the grocery store. "You were asleep!" Gladys says as I open my eyes.

"I didn't realize..."

"Geneva, we have a party to get ready for! Let's go!"

Chocolate, Butter Pecan, Strawberry, Neapolitan, and some crazy flavor called Super Trash were the flavors Gladys and I selected. We ordered a finger food tray full of chicken tenders and wings.

"Do you think this will be enough, Gladys?" I ask.

"I sure hope so, Geneva. We have a herd coming tonight!"

"Sometimes sound brings me back!" I tell her.

"What do you mean, girl?" Gladys asks me. "I hear a certain sound and it brings me back to when I was with him in Pine Mountain, like the wheels of this squeaky cart."

41.

It did bring me back. Pine Mountain had a tiny grocery store.

"He took me there once. When I first walked inside, I got a buggy! The wheels squeaked almost like this cart we're pushing." I say, remembering…

"Come down this aisle, let's pick out a bag of chips." he says.

This store has only five aisles full of all kinds of food. One aisle, the tiniest, had produce and the dairy and eggs. Around the corner it has fresh cut meats from local cows followed by freezer foods.

"Geneva! Hey, Geneva, open your eyes!" Gladys says to me.

I had walked up to her car with my mind in another place. My eyes were closed and the food was already loaded into the trunk-ready to go.

"I was there again!" I say.

Gladys starts her car and drives off. She takes me through a different neighborhood with family houses on both sides of the street. She pointed out to me where her first boyfriend lived long ago.

"That's where he lived. He took me there to meet his parents. It didn't last but a month. Then we split. But, that's the place!" she says.

Back at the home, the residents were arranging the tables in the front atrium for our ice cream social. The tables were covered in light blue plastic table cloths. I help Gladys and a few of our friends from other rooms set the tables with huge plates of finger food and an ocean blue punch bowl.

The entire staff, including all of the kitchen help and cleaning ladies are all in attendance to celebrate the ice cream social this evening. After everyone arrives, a podium is brought out. The director stands up and has everyone help her sing a song. "Welcome, welcome everyone." We start singing. I forget the rest because I hate singing that song. A line forms by the tables. I am third in line to get my finger food and punch. Gladys is helping serve. She thinks I need a rest for the evening since I helped her at the store. I take my plate and punch and find a seat close to the lunch room entrance. It is sort of dark in that corner.

One of the new ladies comes over and sits down beside me.

"I'm Emma!" she tells me.

"I'm Geneva" I say back to her.

"Nice to meet you" she says.

"Same here" I say, chomping down on the still warm chicken tenders.

"My husband was the mayor of this town at one time. I lost him several years ago" she tells me.

I look down at the floor, scrunching up my face. "Honey, what's wrong?" Emma asks.

"I remember something" I say to her, as I swallow a piece of sharp cheddar cheese. "I remember… he and I went to the wooded area. He hated his job back then so we were talking about…

"Honey, I've got to go. It was nice visiting with you!" Emma says as she gets up out of her chair.

Sitting alone at a table, I begin to remember. He and I linger out there at the wooded area until almost midnight.

"I just hate my job. I don't get paid enough and the folks I work with really get on my nerves." Carson says as he lets out a big sigh.

Surely you could find something you would like? There has to be something you could do that would pay more and not stress you so much?"

"I'll find something." he says.

"You could run for mayor!" I say.

He looks over at me in shock.

"I think you would make the perfect mayor! You are quite creative and you know how to get things done." I say, as he laughs at me.

"I wouldn't be mayor of this town for anything. I'm not really interested in that kind of job. It's way too much responsibility!" he says.

"Well, it's just a thought I had, baby!" I say.

He put his arm around me and leans his head down on mine.

"You're the best" he says.

"You're better!" I say back.

The ice in my punch glass has melted and there are only a few stragglers in the room.

"You disappeared on us, Geneva!" Gladys says as she clears the tables.

"I was just eating my finger food. It was great, Gladys." I say as I stand and begin to help her remove the table cloths.

"I had fun tonight, Geneva!" Gladys says.

"Oh I did too. I sat and visited with a new resident." I say.

Gladys turns around and gets the coffee urn. "Would you like some?" she asks.

"I sure would." I tell her.

She pours me a warm cup. We linger over the coffee a few minutes before going to our rooms.

"What a great social" Gladys says.

I think to myself what a wonderful memory! I hope I inspired Carson!

Chapter Nine

He laughs at me after I tell him what a DWK is! I drive him up Commerce Street, making sure to hit every stop sign!

"What is a DWK?" Gladys asks.

"It's a creative way of saying you're Driving While Kissing!"

Gladys laughs at me "Oh!"

"Yes, Gladys, I told him and he thought it was quite funny."

The next morning, I wake up before the sun. I make my way down the quiet hallway into the breakfast room where I make coffee. I make my way through the emptiness of the morning, holding a hot cup in my hands. I find my seat in the atrium, place my cup on the table, and sit watching the maintenance man unlock the sliding doors for the first few cleaning ladies to make their way inside. I sit in my chair and lean my head back, feeling the cool building and the morning chill across my feet. Holding the hot cup in my hands, I think of the winter evening I called him because I needed a friend to talk to.

"Just give me a chance, Carson! You don't even know me as a real person yet, only when I come down. You don't even KNOW me yet, do you?" I scream so loud that night, over the phone, that the neighbors are concerned about me!

"Ok, I'll give you a chance!" he shouts.

"Who is the girl anyway? And what is it about her?" I ask him again.

"She's just a…. friend." he tells me.

"So you're saying I'm enough for you?" I ask.

"Well" Carson answers.

"Well what, Carson?" I ask.

My ring falls off from the anxiety of the whole situation. Sweat was seeping through my shirt as I hung on the hot phone.

"Well, I've got to get ready for work tomorrow. I'll talk to you later." Carson says as he hangs up. 45.

I'll never know what he saw in that girl. The light suddenly comes on in the atrium, waking me up out of a horrible sleep.

"You awake?" a cleaning lady asks me.

"I'm awake. I thought you were Gladys!" I say as she smiles at me.

"Is that yours?" she asks me, pointing to the floor.

My brown pouch had fallen out of my hand and I hadn't realized it.

"Yes, that's mine!" I say as I pick it up. "Thanks" I tell her.

"You're welcome" she says before she continues with her duties.

I take my ring out of the pouch and look at it. It's a reminder of a promise full of hope. It's a preservation of a friendship I'll never forget. Every time I look at it, I can see his smile again. It's a true symbol of a beautiful, most promising new day. A symbol of a journey bright and full of hope.

"Happy Birthday, Geneva." Gladys says after catching me eating a cookie off of the birthday table. Several people have birthdays today and I am one of them.

"Thank you, Gladys!" I say to her as she sits beside me. I almost drop the second cookie into my cup when she startles me.

"How's your morning been, girl?" Gladys asks me.

"Oh, it's ok so far. I had one nightmare and hope the other one waits until I'm ready." I say.

The entertainment director of the home brings in a large box containing a cake with butter crème icing slathered on top and the words 'Happy Birthday' written in blue lettering. "That must be our dessert today." Gladys says, letting out a sigh.

Lunch time is far off. It is only 10:30 and we have a second cup of coffee. I close my eyes again after everyone leaves and heads back into the office for the morning meeting before lunch. I see myself standing in front of his truck.

"I made the right choice, I know I did!" Carson gives me a shameful look. "I KNOW I did, Carson" I say.

He reaches his hand out and places it up against my cheek. He wipes my tears away trying to soothe the great pain in my heart. "I'm not going to accept that!" I tell him again as I start crying. "She's not me." I say.

"You're right." he tells me.

"I love you, always" I tell him, looking into his eyes. "Keep me locked in your heart, ok?"

"I will." he says before pulling out of Chipley Corners.

I open my eyes to find a line forming in the lunchroom. It is almost time to eat and I feel silly sitting there in the same chair from this morning with an empty cup in my hand. I quickly move to put my cup in its proper place, then go to my room and change for lunch. Late again! The line is filtering through the lunchroom past the hot tables. I find Gladys and finally catch up with her. She is getting her chilled fork and knife for her salad. Of course, there is no dessert. It is saved for the big birthday party. They don't want to overload everyone with sugar in here!

"Late again, huh" Gladys looks over at me.

"Yes, Gladys, I am late!" I say while I am reaching for a hot potato.

They have a buffet style meal today. They like to change things up every now and then. I guess to give people the sense of eating out, I don't know. Light piano music is playing in the background. Gladys and I find our seats.

"What did you see when you closed your eyes, Geneva?" Gladys asks as I take our seats in our usual places.

"Carson was telling me about the time he found another girl. I told him he's making a terrible mistake!"

Gladys shook her head "Sounds drab."

"I know. It was when it happened. I really thought it was just some kind of joke he and Thomas thought up." I say as I begin to eat.

"Look at it this way, Geneva. It's not your worry now!" Gladys says as she smiles while she cuts a piece of steak.

My heart feels heavy today after those dreams I had this morning. My mind is numb and my joints hurt me badly. The birthday party is interesting! The director has everyone's attention in the room. She is holding a piece of paper with the names of the five residents who have a birthday today. I was the last one called before everyone sings happy birthday to us. We are called up for the first few slices of cake! The director asks all of us to turn around and face the crowd. Everyone applauds us! I look over to see Gladys with a happy look on her face. The cook drops a big piece of dark chocolate cake on my cool plate. The blue rose turns into a blue blob but it is still a rose. Returning to the table, I sit down and tell Gladys.

"I almost went back again in my mind. But it was a good memory."

"Girl, tell me over coffee!" she says.

The cake is delicious! It was made by a local bakery out of an old recipe book. It tastes like the cupcakes my mom used to buy from the grocery cake case years ago.

"Tell you what, Geneva, let's go get coffee at the place down the road from here!" Gladys says, as we put our empty plates on the tray for disposal. "Let me go grab my keys!" She says, as she hurries to her room.

I wait out in the atrium in the same seat I started out in this morning. The only thing is, I try not to close my eyes. Another memory would return in a nightmare!

"You ready?" Gladys says to me, as she is digging through her purse hunting for her keys.

"Ready!" I say, following her out the doors.

"I just had to get out of this place for the afternoon! I hope you feel like hanging at a coffee shop?" Gladys asks.

"Oh I do, Gladys!" I say to her.

I try all day not to think about anything but the great birthday lunch I had and the delicious cake afterwards. I tell Gladys to keep talking in the car, I don't want to reminisce.

Taking a seat in the tiny crowded coffee shop, she and I wait on two large cups of steaming hot hazelnut truffle coffee with whipped cream on top.

"So tell me about you going back again." she says.

"Oh, the dream I had?" I say.

"Yes, the one you wanted to tell me at lunch?" Gladys says.

I close my eyes. The sun came out all of a sudden, illuminating the coffee shop. It brought me back to that summer day in May. I was with him in the gardens, holding his hand.

"Geneva!" Gladys said startling me. "Geneva, tell me about your dream" she says.

I relax in my chair again. "I remember this, Gladys. I walked with him through the gardens that May."

"He took me down to the beach area. The Gardens symphony was playing! He grabs my hands and spins me around and around and around. I am dying in endless laughter on a warm summer evening!" I say.

"Coffee's ready, be right back!" Gladys says to me, as she gets up to get our coffee. I close my eyes again to see us stopped at the small cement bridge. "Is there anything that ever goes on here?" I ask.

"Not too much in Pine Mountain. I just come out here and hike the trails or rent a bicycle to ride down the paths." he says.

He lets go of my hand and grabs a quarter out of his pocket to buy some feed for the many turtles that live in the pond.

"Come here, I'll show you something." Carson says, after pouring feed into my hands.

He walks me over to the edge of the bridge and throws about five balls of feed into the water. All of a sudden the water starts moving and thousands of turtles emerge from the deep area, making a popping sound as I look on in amazement.

"That's Bob, Slick, Pop and Old Man." he says, naming all of the turtles.

I look at him and start smiling.

"What?" he asks me.

"You are remarkable!" I say.

My heart starts racing again as he holds his arms out for me.

"Come here." he says.

I'm smothered tightly in his arms. I see him frown slightly.

49.

"What's wrong?" I ask him.

"Oh, nothing." he says.

"I don't care if you never let me go. I want to be here forever because I'm comfortable." I say as he leans his head down on mine.

"I know!" he says.

"Hey!" I hear Gladys say to me as I open my eyes.

"Are you going to wake up? Your coffee's getting cold." she says.

"Oh yeah." I say, as I open my eyes to reality.

"You were just sitting there mumbling. I thought you were going to tell me about your dream?" she says to me.

"I thought I did. I was certainly there again!" I say.

Gladys rolls her eyes and we don't speak for the rest of the evening. It's frustrating sometimes, knowing you have these flashbacks and really want them to be your reality. Maybe they will again.

That night in my sleep, I have a vivid dream. Carson takes me downtown. At the end of the row of buildings is a tiny ice cream shop.

"It's where people go in the summertime to cool off!" Carson says, as he smiles while he is driving me up to the place.

"I'll get you some ice cream." he says, as he parks and gets out of his truck.

The ice cream shop is the last shop on the street in downtown Pine Mountain. Walking in, there is a large case with many flavors of ice cream. Of course, he chose his favorite, Superman.

"I think YOU are superman!" I say to him, laughing.

He laughs and says "Get what you want."

I look around at all the flavors and then I look over into a case filled with fudge.

"That's what I want, right there" I point to a huge slab of chocolate pecan fudge. It is home-made from a local fudge maker. Carson buys two bottles of water from Pine Mountain's local spring. It has a crisp smooth flavor and it's very energizing!

50.

"Oh, Carson, I love you!" I say to him, giving him a hug as he is paying.

We sit at a small table outside. We can't stop smiling and making eyes at each other. We talk a lot and make plans for our future. He can't stop smiling at me. After finishing our treats, we get up and walk back to his truck. Grabbing my waist, he pulls me over and around for a cold wet kiss-one that gives me chills because his lips are so cold!

I wake up. It's morning back at the home. The distant sounds of downtown Pine Mountain are still ringing in my ears as I make my way to the library before breakfast. I think a good book will keep my mind off nightmares and flashbacks! I find a simple but exciting story. I can't put it down for a week!

Chapter Ten

"So what caused you two to be at odds, Geneva?" Gladys asks me.

She and I are enjoying a wonderful breakfast.

"One of his best friends seems to have influenced his decision." I say. "His friend, Thomas, convinced him that I was not right for him. Carson decided to go for another girl. That's what he told me at the time"

Gladys wrinkles up her forehead as she sits down at the table. It is almost Christmas and I start remembering the good times I had with Carson.

"Have I told you about Christmas in Pine Mountain, Gladys? He took me out to the annual light show out at Callaway Gardens."

"Nope" Gladys replies.

"He invited me to come down to see the annual Christmas lights. Of course, I couldn't wait to see him. I had his gifts in the back of my car."

Gladys knocks her cup against the table. "There's no cream in my coffee! I forgot the creamer!"

A song is playing in the breakfast room. It is one I haven't heard since I was out at the light show. "'Sleigh Ride' was one of the songs playing the night we were there!" I say.

Gladys turns around quickly. "What?" she asks with a look of question on her face.

"'Sleigh Ride' was the song playing out at Callaway Gardens when we walked up to get a gingerbread cookie and some hot cocoa."

Gladys is quick to smile as she sits down. "Tell me more about your Christmas experience with him." Gladys says.

"It happened like this." I say. "There was a parade that afternoon in his little town. I had to be there early."

"You were in a parade?" Gladys asks me.

"Yes I was… with him."

The floats are lining up downtown. It is the annual Christmas parade in Pine Mountain. He and I are on a horse drawn carriage. Everyone claps as we pass them because it looks so authentic.

"That's incredible!" Gladys says to me with a smile.

After the parade, we stop by Gayla's Gift Shop. After saying 'Hi' to Gayla, Carson takes me to a little bakery down the sidewalk.

"They have the best buttermilk croissants here." he says as he holds the door for me.

We walk into this tiny bakery and restaurant. The smell of bread baking and the scent of many spices engulf us.

"How many in your party"? The man at the counter asks across the busy dining room.

"Just two!" Carson answers.

The man grabs two menus from behind the host stand and guides us around the corner to a table set for four. The table is wooden with a red and white striped table cloth. The menus are printed on multi colored paper

I order hot mulling cider. It comes in a carafe.

"Here, Carson, have some cider" I say as I pour cider into a cup.

We order two breakfasts with country ham and sausage. We order two buttermilk croissants instead of biscuits.

"Keep talking." Gladys says.

"We finish eating. I sip the last of my cider and we leave for the light show." I tell her.

December's chill greets us. He takes me out to Callaway Gardens after our wonderful time downtown. Cars are lined up, ready to drive through the lights. We get out and walk up to the concessions. The smell of fresh baked gingerbread and the occasional whiff of hot cocoa fills the air that cool night. The song, 'Sleigh Ride' is playing. Carson holds my hand.

"Let's go inside and see what's going on in here" he says, entering a giant red and white striped tent.

We walk into the tent. An enormous crowd is lined up for pictures with Santa. At tables kids can create Christmas ornaments and build toys to give as gifts. He walks me all the way to the back. Gingerbread cookies and hot chocolate are for sale as well as cakes and delicious pies.

"They have a circus here in the summer." Carson says to me.

"Really?" I ask him.

"Yep, and you and I will come see it next summer." he promises.

We have five minutes to drink our hot cocoa. I bought two candy canes for a photo op. We hold the two candy canes together, making the shape of a heart.

"Of course, someone took our picture and it was cute!" I say

Gladys looks up at me.

"So, how was the light show?" she asks me.

"It was great!" I say. "They have it every year!"

All of a sudden, I close my eyes and I'm there, sitting in his truck. We start moving in the line. A man with a light stick is directing traffic. A sign says "Christmas Lights" and we turn in the direction the arrow points. The long road leads us through many giant toy soldiers on each side of the road. He laughs at the music coming out of the speakers.

"They've had this for years and it never changes!" He told me as we drive through the lighted scenes.

Gladys finishes the last sip of coffee out of her cup.

"The light show drive lasted about an hour." I tell her. "It is the most wonderful experience I've had in a long time!"

Gladys carefully washes her cup at the sink and places it on the top counter ready for next time's use.

"We saw all the lights and then drove out of them.

"What happened next?" Gladys asks.

"He took me to a little white church out in the country. It was down a dirt road. We sat out there and looked at all of the stars, counting every one of them."

"I always get a little teary eyed remembering my wonderful trip." I say.

Gladys came over and patted me on the back.

"It's ok, Geneva. You had a beautiful experience with him that you'll never forget!"

....

"I get concerned when you don't answer!" I tell him.

I am in Pine Mountain for the annual festival. Many artists and crafters line the street.The shops are decked out in their finest and all of the folks who were staying at the gardens are curious about the big event.

"I was busy that day. So I couldn't talk." Carson says.

"Oh" I say as I help a guest who walks up to my table.

"I was really worried about you, though!" I said.

"I know!" he says back to me.

"Come here." he says as he holds his arm out. I lean over and give him a hug.

"He had a sparkle in his eye like nothing I've ever seen before, Gladys!"

I say to her as she is driving over the bridge in town.

"So you two hung out there all day?" Gladys asks me with a smile.

"Yes, I was working at the festival!"

"After the festival, he walked me down to the mural. It was behind an antique store! It had to be hand painted. He told me it was painted in 3D!" I say to Gladys.

"Anyway you look at the painting, it follows you!" Carson says. "And look over there down that road. This town used to have rail road tracks. That's where the train would stop."

"Interesting!" I say as I look in the direction he points.

The sounds of downtown mix with the September breeze and the smell of hot dogs and baked goods.

With his warm hearted smile, he looks over at me and says, "We'll do all of this over again when we get hitched!"

"Gladys, I just close my eyes and I can actually smell the sweet scent coming from the shops. I can taste the coffee served at the country store. I know if I go there again it won't be anything like I remember. The brick criss-crossed sidewalk, the fountain in the square -none of that may be there anymore. If I ever have a chance again. I'll re-live walking down the red brick sidewalks and eating at the small restaurant downtown."

"Geneva!" Gladys says.

"I know, Gladys, I'm dwelling again!" I say.

"Did I tell you, I only met his parents twice?" I tell her.

"You never brought it up, but why only twice?" she asked.

"I really never knew why, I couldn't wait to be family with them. You know, I loved him very much. It made me sad."

Gladys wrinkles her forehead and looks at me sadly. "Sometimes you don't understand why things like that happen, Geneva." she says.

"I guess so, Gladys!" I reply.

She is right. I let out a big sigh and rest my fingers on the warm coffee cup I have sitting on the small coffee table beside the lunchroom entrance. I close my eyes for just a second.

"Shh!" Carson stops me and says "Listen!"

"What is it, baby?" I ask.

"I thought I heard something." he says.

We are out on the trail in the wooded area and it is cold.

"Catch me if you can!" I say as I take off running.

"Hey!" he hollers.

I run just as fast as I can, up over the hill, nearly slipping on a loose patch of leaves. I hide behind a giant tree.

"CATCH ME IF YOU CAN!" I shout as I stand still and wait. I am there about a minute. I peep from behind the tree, and am startled by a tall guy saying "Found You!"

"You startled me, you know!" I say.

"You scared me, you know!" he says back to me as he winks.

My heart is still racing from running and being startled. He wraps his arms around me and props his head on mine.

"Your heart is racing." he says.

56.

"Are you cold?" he asks.

"No, I'm quite warm and comfy in your arms." I say.

He kisses me and props his chin on the top of my head again.

"Carson?"

"Hmm?" he answers.

"I love you." I say. I take my icy cold fingers and caress his cheeks.

I open my eyes to find myself still sitting in my chair by the lunchroom entrance. I take my cup of stale coffee back to the breakfast room. I turn the light on and pour my icy coffee into the sink, wash my cup and set it right by Gladys'.

I do not see Gladys the rest of the evening. She must be visiting with other friends. I want to tell her about the dream I had. Maybe later I will. I sit in the breakfast room a while and...I close my eyes.

"You seem distant" I say, while looking at him. "What's wrong, Carson?" I ask, as I nibble my grilled cheese sandwich.

We are sitting outside, at the tables, by the Discovery Center at Callaway Gardens.

"Nothing" he answers.

"Are you sure? I ask.

"Yeah" he answers with a halfhearted smile.

I know something isn't right, so I dig a little deeper.

"Really, tell me what's bothering you." I say

"I've found someone else!" he answers.

The shockwave hit me. Suddenly the grilled cheese sandwich turns stale and my heart sinks deep into my chest.

"I don't believe you." I say to him.

He never smiled after telling me. He just sat there in silence. I gather up the greasy napkins, placing them in the still warm basket containing a half-eaten sandwich and put an empty water cup on top of all of it, then throw it away. He is right behind me, not saying much.

"I'm sorry, Geneva!" He says as we are walking back to his truck.

"Why?" I ask him as I turn around.

"What did I do"? I ask.

"Why do you think it's you?" he says to me.

I hug him this time longer and tighter than ever. I'm glad I did, because that would be one of the last times I hugged him, but I didn't know it yet.

The next day, I speak to Gladys about what is troubling me. It's this memory that keeps circling around in my head and I can't get it out.

"What was I supposed to do about it, Gladys?" I ask, as we are shopping.

"Not much, girl. What could you have done to change it?" she asks me.

"I really don't know. I just didn't see it coming" I say.

I take a seat on the brown wooden bench outside of the dress store in the mall. I look around me and see all of the happy families.

I sit there while the world passes by in this busy place. Gladys finally comes out with a few bags in her hands.

"I'm done here!" she says. "Let's go find the others and get on the bus."

Gladys and I walk through the mall and out the double doors.

"Oh, Geneva, I forgot my glasses! I left them on the counter back at the dress shop. Can you hold on to these? I'll be back in a flash!"

"Sure, Gladys" I say. I take the three bags Gladys hands me and head toward the ride home. Of course, I hate group trips. We usually ended up sitting on the bus for about 45 minutes, waiting on the rest of the good folks. The seats are soft though, I do have to say that much.

"Everybody on board" The driver hollers as he steps up into the cab. Everyone shouts at the same time "YEAH" The brake is released and we start rolling. We are on our way back to the home for the rest of the evening.

Back at the home, I walk to the rec room where. I join in for a few rounds of exercise. Then, I go to the breakfast room for a few minutes. I read through the newspaper.

Something is odd at the home this evening- Gladys is missing!

Walking up front, I realize what must have happened! We left Gladys at the mall! The director goes immediately to get her. We are all glad to see her when she returns.

It has been a long day. I close my eyes at the dinner table, not speaking to anyone around me. After dinner, I quickly head to my bed. I hear a knock at the door. It's probably Gladys or someone checking on me, I think, as I drift into an exhausted sleep.

In my dream I'm running… As fast as I can on a misty morning I run all the way from downtown to the gas station- half a mile; I'm yelling…

"Carson! Carson! Wait!" But I can't catch up to him.

The mist and fog gets thicker in Pine Mountain as I keep running and running- eventually making it to the Chipley Corners station. The parking lot is empty. The doors are closed tightly. No one is there. I look around me.

I shout "CARSON!" But no one can hear me.

And then it is morning.

Chapter Eleven

This is a strange dream. I'm climbing down a ladder into a water flow with a dirt bottom. All of a sudden, out of nowhere, a big gush of water knocks me over. It spins me around and all I can see is red dirt. I open my eyes to vaguely see someone standing at the bottom.

"Who are you?" I ask

An arm reaches out for me and pulls me from the strong current.

"I am your destiny!" the person says.

Still, I could not see who this is. I have dirt in my eyes and can't see very well. The person pulls me in closer.

"Still don't recognize me?" he asks.

"No!" I reply.

"Well, come here." the stranger says, pulling me closer. "You know who I am- unless you've forgotten?"

He leans his head on mine. He locks his hands in place around my waist bringing a familiar comfort.

"I am your destiny!" the person says.

I look up at the tall figure. It's Carson! I start to cry as he holds me closer in his arms.

"You rescued me from a dangerous current!" I tell him.

"Remember when I told you, I would always be there for you?" Carson asks.

"Yes!" I say.

"You were in trouble, so I came to your rescue. I heard you screaming." he says.

"I remember, Carson!" I say to him.

He holds me close in his arms until I can breathe again. All of a sudden, water starts swirling around stirring red dirt into my eyes and I lose sight of Carson. The current takes me down the water flow. Before I hit the side of the wall…

"Ding!" "Ding!" The morning bell jolts me awake!

It's the day of the convention on aging. I am not looking forward to this long day. I sit up in bed and lift my heavy legs down to slide my feet into my house slippers. I dress and walk down to the breakfast room to find Gladys.

"You ready to hop on the bus?" We have a two hour ride to the event." she asks as I make my way over to get a cup of coffee.

"I'm ready, Gladys, as ready as I'll ever be!" I say.

I only have one cup of coffee and two mini doughnuts with white powdered sugar. Gladys and I are the last ones to board the bus.

"Is it comfy enough for you, Geneva?" she asks me with a smile.

"I'm ok, I guess!" I tell her as I re-adjust myself in the seat. "I dread these trips!" I say, looking over at Gladys.

"Me too, girl. I can't really take it myself, but hey! They want us to go, so we are going!" she says.

The bus eventually starts moving. "Here we go!" Gladys mumbles as we turn out of the home parking lot.

I lean my head back against the seat and close my eyes.

"Hey, baby! I have a little surprise for you. Are you ready?" I ask Carson over the phone.

"Sure, what is it?" he asks me.

"I'm in Warm Springs and I'll be in Pine Mountain in about ten minutes!" I say.

"I got sneaky on you didn't I?" I say.

"You sure did!" he says.

I park my car in the parking lot beside an antique store. I get out and fill my lungs with the warm spring air. "I'll see you in about ten minutes!" I tell him before hanging up. "I love you!" I say. "I love you too!" he says back.

I walk into the antique store to get a crystal arrowhead for him. I hurry out the door and get in my car and head to Pine Mountain for the start of a near perfect day! My ring sparkles in the sun and shadow as I drive under the thick pine trees over the road. Nearing my destination, I pass beside the Liberty Bell Pool. I take a right at the light beside Chipley Corners and head toward downtown.

Then I see him, sitting in his truck, waiting for me! My heart races in excitement! I pull up beside him and jump out. He picks me up and spins me around. "Oh, it's so good to see you, Carson!" I say, putting my ear up to his chest to listen to his heart. "I've missed you!" he says as he smiles.

I climb into his truck to find his dog waiting for me, wagging her tail! I close the door. My heart is racing…

"Geneva… Geneva, we're here!" Gladys shouts, nudging me out of sleep. "We're here. Everyone's getting off. Let's go, girl!" she says as I open my eyes.

"I'm here." I mumble. Gladys can't hear me. I get up out of my seat and catch up with her. I am the last one off.

Walking into the giant hotel, I see many seniors from around the state. Everyone has custom name tags showing their names and where they're from. Gladys and I eventually find each other and make our way into the huge auditorium. Our residents sit in one single section.

"Here we go!" Gladys tells me, taking her seat. These meetings last hours and are never exciting.

"We'll get through it!" I tell her, taking my seat and leaning my head back.

The lights dim and the curtain opens to reveal a panel of five experts waiting to answer questions. Gladys and I usually close our eyes through it and fall asleep until the end. The best part of the convention is always the huge buffet that is served!

We arrive back at the home after midnight. Exhausted, I stumble to my room and fall into a deep sleep.

I wake up from a nightmare. Everything went terribly wrong that afternoon!

I hurry to breakfast and tell Gladys my nightmare.

"Why won't you date me?" Thomas asks, leering at me then looking over at his friend Carson.

"Someone has my heart..... That's why..." I answer. I was shocked at his boldness! I would never betray Carson!

"Was this the second fuss you had with him?" Gladys asks me.

"No, the third..." I say. "I never gave up on Carson because I always knew who I loved!"

"Hi, Geneva!" George says as he walks over to the counter where he pours a cup of coffee.

"Hey, George" I say back to him "Make yourself at home."

He sits down across from me, propping his cane up against the wall. "What kind of trouble are you into today?" George asks me.

"Oh not too much, I'm just sitting here remembering." I tell him.

George removes his glasses and lays them on the table. "Remembering?" he asks.

"Yes, I was remembering the day when Carson and I had a fuss." I say.

The seasons were changing in Pine Mountain and I was in town for the weekend.

"Oh see me now? Into the fields of golden love I go... I am there in my mind where my heart rests on still waters. I found you there. The distant sun catches your eye. Your gentle smile warms my heart as you reach for me inside your dreams. Do you like it, Carson?" I say to him as we pull up to the Ridge.

"Yes, it's very nice!" he says to me.

"I wrote that last night- part of a song I'm thinking about." I say.

As we get out of his truck, he takes my hand and leads me down a leaf covered path to an enormous grey rock!

"Here I am now, sitting right beside my future wife!" Carson smiles as he puts his arm around me. We have the most beautiful view, looking out across Pine Mountain Valley. We can see a factory in the distance. It makes a picturesque ornament in the scenery as white smoke billows out of its smoke pipes into the brilliant blue sky. The breeze brushes against the treetops as a little grey bird catches our attention.

"Look at that, Carson! Isn't that pretty? God sent us a song!"

"Yep, that's pretty." he says to me. "You know, Geneva, I haven't lost my spark for you, I think I never will." Carson says smiling, looking into my eyes. I put my arms around him and give him a tight hug. "I never will either, Carson. You're the best."

The little grey chickadee sings to us until we head back to the truck. On the road back to town, his phone rings. It is Thomas. He wants to meet us at the Chipley Corners station in Pine Mountain. Carson says Thomas has something to tell me. I am curious.

"Well, go ahead and tell us!" Gladys says to me as she looks around the breakfast room.

I had no idea that an hour had already passed. The breakfast hour was almost at an end. Gladys pulls her chair closer to the table.

"It happened like this." I say.

Thomas met us up at the Chipley Corners. "Hey, man!" Carson greets Thomas out the window of his truck. Thomas waves at Carson as he walks across the hot asphalt of the tiny parking lot.

He leans in to the window on my side of the truck.

"Ok, Geneva, so here's the thing going on right now." Thomas says to me. "Carson has been seeing another woman and I think he has already made his choice. Am I making myself clear?"

I am completely shocked. I looked over at Carson and asked him "Carson is this true?"

He sits there in his truck, his head bowed. "Give the ring back to Carson, Geneva!" Thomas demands.

My eyes began to get moist..." I…. I'm keeping the ring, Thomas…"

"WHY?" he shouts.

"It's the only thing I have that is truly from Carson's heart. I am going to treasure this ring forever, just like I promised when he gave it to me." I say.

"Ok, Geneva, you can keep the damn thing!" Carson says. Thomas looks at me and laughs out loud.

"Let's go!" Thomas urges Carson.

I remember I didn't spend enough time with Carson that day. The perfect day just became a disaster.

"I'm going to really miss you this time." I tell him as I get out of his truck "I love you!" I say as I slam the door.

"I love you too!" he tells me as I look back at him.

I thought about it later… "How did that happen?" I ask myself as I drive off the parking lot of Chipley Corner.

The lunch bell rings. "Five minutes till lunch- we'd better head down!" Gladys says.

George grabs his cane and starts down the hall. Gladys and I tag behind.

"So his friend had a role in the break up?" Gladys asks me.

"So it seemed!" I say.

All three of us sit down for lunch at the cloth covered table. "So I wonder, Geneva, did you ever go back to Pine Mountain?" Gladys asks me, as she is being served her roasted lemon pepper chicken.

"Actually, Gladys, I did go back once after that. But if I had known going down to Pine Mountain would cause us to lose touch that day, I would never have gone back then."

"What do you mean, Geneva?" Gladys asks.

George starts eating his lemon pepper chicken. I could tell he was listening closely. He took a sip of his tea and looks me right in the eye.

"It's not easy to talk about, Gladys. I still have thoughts of him. I will tell you exactly what happened….."

Chapter Twelve

It lived with me for many years, what happened on that hot summer day in June. I came to see him... a two and a half hour trip in the middle of June. He had invited me to go swimming with him at Callaway Gardens!

Carson lets me know he is at Gayla's Gift Shop and to meet him there. Excited, I drive up to the shop.

I arrive to see him in the heart of downtown Pine Mountain. I park and get out of my car. I glance upward at the beautiful American flag waving in the wind against the bright blue sky. The sound of a fountain makes a musical tune as I walk across the street to Gayla's.

His voice echoes out of the tiny screen door as I wander up the sidewalk. I see him. His face smiles, and then is quick to turn into a frown as he walks out the door of the tiny shop. His friend Thomas follows him outside.

"It's over" Carson says.

The smile I had saved for him quickly leaves my face. The happiness of the day turns into a nightmare.

As Carson exits the tiny building, the afternoon sun glitters on him, making his brown eyes look as delectable as a cream soda on a hot summer day. His mouth is turned downward as his friend Thomas comes out of the shop and stands between us.

Lighting a cigarette, Thomas begins to speak. He makes it very clear to me how offended he is that I called him on the phone one night wondering if he knew where Carson was?

"I can't see through the phone" I say…

"I don't understand you" Thomas hollers at me, his dark sunglasses hanging on his nose like they were glued there.

Sweet Mrs. Gayla came running out of her shop asking "What's going on?"

Thomas answers, "We can't get Geneva to understand!"

"Carson and I are supposed to be swimming. What happened"? I ask.

"Carson!" Thomas turns and looks at him.

Carson looks sheepish. His body is half in the shade and half in the sunshine. He rolls his eyes and looks upward.

"Tell her, Carson! Tell her!" Thomas shouts.

Carson sighs, and then mumbles that he is in a relationship with another girl.

He turns and walks quickly to his truck and slams the door. After nearly three years of a long enduring friendship it is officially broken… gone…. over!

"I still get teary eyed when you ask me about what happened. All I can say is I loved him very much and I hope to see him again one day." I say.

"So you never saw him again, Geneva?"

Gladys looks down at her meal and frowns sadly.

"No, Gladys." I say. "Yet, I still think of him."

Gladys asks me, "Have you tried looking him up?"

"No." I answer. "I'm afraid. Since that day, I've just been too afraid of what he might say or do. I just haven't had the courage to go to Pine Mountain and look for him, but I always wonder what happened to him."

Gladys pushes her chair away from the table and gets up to take her plate to the cafeteria window. She edges over to me and puts her hand on my shoulder and says,

"If I were you, I would go get the wonder out of your heart. Even if you never find him, even if he's moved away, I would at least go spend a few days there to find out what happened to him. That would make things better for you."

"I guess it would, Gladys." I say.

"Try it, girl. At least go see." Gladys says.

"The thought of going back gives me butterflies... "I'll do it!" I say!

I did everything we used to do many years ago. I go to the wooded area and walk the path under bare branched trees. I drive up to the Chipley Corners gas station and see the blinding white asphalt is still here. I drive past Callaway Gardens and enjoy the view. I drive up to the lookout to find that the restaurant is still here. I follow the two lane road back into downtown Pine Mountain. The fountain is still here. The shops are here but different. The brick criss-crossed sidewalk is still here.

I park and step out of my car. The air is crisp and cold- the dead of winter in a small West Georgia town. Walking into a shop, I notice a picture on the wall. I walk over and calmly ask the clerk,

"Who is that man in that picture hanging above your mantle?"

"The Mayor." the clerk replies.

"Oh!" I say as my heart starts racing.

I hurriedly purchase a piece of old fashioned fudge.

I pay for my item then walk towards the exit. Before I close the door behind me, I ask the clerk,

"Where do I find him?"

"City Hall, it's the building on the next street." the clerk replies.

"Thank you" I say as I hurry out the door!

A light rain is falling in Pine Mountain as I pull up to the small red brick building. The windows are clear and shiny. There is a small curtain slightly pulled back for light. The door looks heavy and firm as I walk up and open it.

"Good afternoon ma'am. May I help you?" the secretary asks.

"Yes, I'm here to see the Mayor!"

I walk in hesitantly. My heart is beating a thousand times a minute.

"Have a seat. He'll be with you in a moment." she says.

I walk over to the leather covered chairs and sit, quietly looking at all of the old railroad décor displayed in the office. The light through the windows sinks into a buttery glow.

"What brings you here to see the mayor?" the girl asks me.

"I'm sure the mayor is a long lost friend of mine whom I lost touch with years ago." I say.

"Excuse me!" the girl says as she answers the phone.

I sit there forever in anticipation, watching the girl at the desk go about her job. She seems to have forgotten all about me.

Dozens of welcome brochures are placed in the waiting room magazine rack for visitors to enjoy. The one with the butterflies printed on the front catches my eye.

A noise comes from his office and his secretary informs me to go in to see him. I walk into the room where he sits. His office is dark with books against the wall on my left. His desk has papers scattered all over it. There he is, sitting in his chair, writing on cream colored paper. He looks at me.

"How can I help you today?" he asks me.

I don't think he recognizes me.

I sit down quietly in the soft leather chair in front of his enormous desk, careful not to make any noise. He clears his throat.

As he is searching through his paperwork, I say....

"Well!"

I take the sparkling Destiny Ring out of its special pouch and click it on the glassy desk top. Then I say to the Mayor…

"I hope you have kept me locked in your heart. I hope no one has ever been able to take me out of it because you were my best friend and I came all the way down here today to tell you that you still are!"

The mayor stops looking through his papers. He places the pen on his desk and leans back in his chair. "Geneva?" he whispers with a shocked look on his face.

"Geneva!" he says in shock.

"Yes, it's me" I say as tears start welling up in my eyes.

He takes his glasses off and wipes his eyes. He is speechless! After all, it has only been thirty years since we've seen each other.

"Geneva… I can't believe it's you." Carson says.

"Geneva, I never forgot you"

"Do you remember that I promised to you long ago, Carson? I would always treasure this ring?" I asked him.

"And you still have it?!" he asks.

"I still have it! I never could part with it. It's the only thing I have that is truly from your heart. I thought if I ever parted with it, the world would end."

"And I told you to keep it" Carson answers.

"And I did!" I say as I smile at him.

"I can't believe it!" he says.

We sit in the silence of his office in the shock and amazement of our meeting.

"How did you find me?" Carson asks.

"I saw your picture hanging in a store. So I asked and the clerk told me where you were" I say.

He glances down at the ring sitting on his desk.

"You told me something before, Geneva, and I always remembered it" he says.

"Keep me locked in your heart…." I reply.

"And never let anyone take me out of it" he finished softly.

"Well, have you"? I ask him.

He looks into my eyes and smiles. "I never could" he says.

"I love you, Carson" I say.

The Destiny Ring.

Printed in Poland
by Amazon Fulfillment
Poland Sp. z o.o., Wrocław